Weather
Seasons

For Iris Holloway

Look out for:
Kitten Cat

Scholastic Children's Books
Commonwealth House, 1-19 New Oxford Street
London WC1A 1NU, UK
a division of Scholastic Ltd
London ~ New York ~ Toronto ~ Sydney ~ Auckland
Mexico City ~ New Delhi ~ Hong Kong

First published in hardback in the UK by Scholastic Ltd, 2004

Copyright © Ian Beck, 2004

ISBN 0 439 97719 3

Printed in Singapore

2 4 6 8 10 9 7 5 3 1

Kitten Cat
Rainy Day Play

Ian Beck

SCHOLASTIC
PRESS

'Oh dear, it's raining,' says Mother Cat.
'You'd better stay in and play today, Kitten Cat.'
Kitten Cat looks out into the garden.
'Mew,' he says.

Kitten Cat watches the raindrops on the window. He tries to stop one, and then another, and another but he can't.
'Mew, mew,' says Kitten Cat.

Then Kitten Cat runs fast, round and round the table leg, but he slips over spilling a saucer of milk all over the floor.

Kitten Cat climbs on to a table with his wet
paws and leaves messy little paw prints.

He reaches for his favourite toy.

Kitten Cat carries the toy to the edge
of the table. 'Careful,' says Mother Cat.
'Mew,' says Kitten Cat.

Kitten Cat throws the
toy on to the floor.
It lands with a big
SQUEAK!
'Mew, mew,' says
Kitten Cat.
'Not too noisy now,'
says Mother Cat.

Kitten Cat jumps down and picks up the toy.
It makes a little squeak.
'Quietly now,' says Mother Cat.

Kitten Cat puts the toy down. He looks at Mother Cat, and squeezes the toy and makes another squeak. 'Remember, sshh,' says Mother Cat.

Kitten Cat jumps as hard as he can on to the toy. It makes a very loud SQUEAK!

Mother Cat takes the toy away.

'I did ask you to be quiet,' says Mother Cat.

Kitten Cat cries.

Mother Cat gives him a big hug.
'The rain is stopping!' she says. 'Let's go outside.'

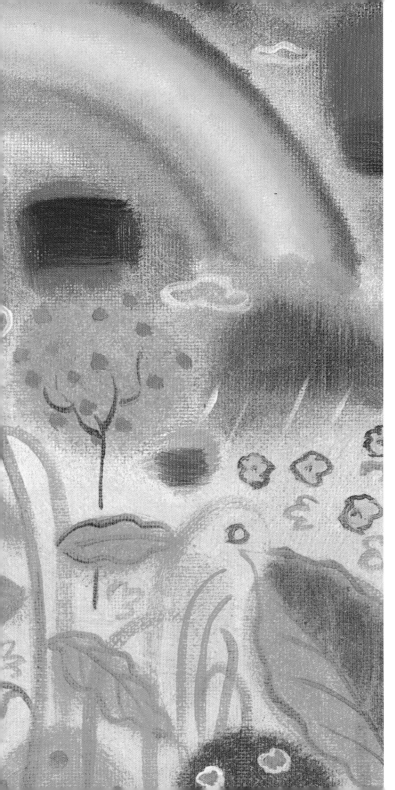

'Look,' says Mother Cat,
'a rainbow!'
'Miaow,' says Kitten Cat.
'Purrrr, purrrr, purrr.'